The Chronicles of MEAP

MEAP!

ADAPTED BY JOHN GREEN

BASED ON THE SERIES CREATED BY
DAN POVENMIRE & JEFF "SWAMPY" MARSH

DISNEY PRESS

NEW YORK

LIBRARY OF CONGRESS CATALOG CARD NUMBER ON FILE.
ISBN 978-1-4231-2441-2
FIRST EDITION
10 9 8 7 6 5 4 3 2 1
PRINTED IN THE UNITED STATES OF AMERICA
H886-4759-0-10105

FOR MORE DISNEY PRESS FUN, VISIT WWW.DISNEYBOOKS.COM
VISIT DISNEYCHANNEL.COM

SUMMER VACATION! THERE'S A WHOLE LOT OF STUFF TO DO BEFORE SCHOOL STARTS, AND *PHINEAS* AND *FERB* PLAN TO DO IT ALL! MAYBE THEY'LL BUILD A ROCKET, OR FIND FRANKENSTEIN'S BRAIN...WHATEVER THEY DO, THEY'RE SURE TO ANNOY THEIR SISTER, *CANDACE.* MEANWHILE, THEIR FAMILY PET, *PERRY* THE PLATYPUS, LEADS A DOUBLE LIFE AS *AGENT P,* FACING OFF AGAINST THE DEVIOUS *DR. DOOFENSHMIRTZ!*

The Chronicles of MEAP

IT'S THE BOTTOM OF THE NINTH INNING. BASES ARE LOADED. IT ALL COMES DOWN TO THIS FINAL PITCH FROM FERB "THE CURVE" FLETCHER.

HERE'S THE WINDUP...

POOMF!

AND IT'S A STEEERIII--

veep veep

--IIIII--

--IIIKE! AND THE CROWD GOES WILD!

THERE'S THE LESSON, BASEBALL FANS--NEVER JUDGE A BOOK BY ITS COVER.

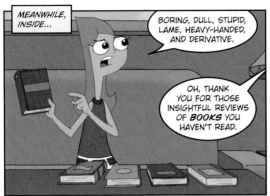

MEANWHILE, INSIDE...

BORING, DULL, STUPID, LAME, HEAVY-HANDED, AND DERIVATIVE.

OH, THANK YOU FOR THOSE INSIGHTFUL REVIEWS OF *BOOKS* YOU HAVEN'T READ.

MOM, THAT'S WHY BOOKS HAVE COVERS-- TO *JUDGE* THEM. I MEAN, WHY DID YOU CHOOSE *THESE* BOOKS FROM THE LIBRARY?

THEY...LOOKED INTERESTING...

SO...

POINT TAKEN.

OKAY, HONEY, I'M OFF TO HELP DAD AT THE ANTIQUE STORE.

OOH, HEY, HERE'S A PACKAGE FOR YOU!

MY BANGO-RU!

YOUR WHAT?

MY BANGO-RU! THEY'RE THESE ADORABLE JAPANESE CHARACTERS THAT ARE SO *IN* RIGHT NOW. LIKE, IN A KITSCHY WAY.

THE GUITARIST FOR THE BETTYS HAS ONE PAINTED ON HER GUITAR! STACY AND I DESIGNED OUR OWN DOLLS ONLINE.

WELL, ASSUMING NONE OF THAT IS TEENAGE CODE FOR SOMETHING I SHOULD BE WORRIED ABOUT AS A PARENT, I'M OFF.

BYE, MOM! I'M GONNA CALL STACY!

BANGO-RU!

BANGO-RU! I JUST GOT MY LITTLE BUNNY-BEAR! IT'S A CROSS BETWEEN A BUNNY AND A BEAR. YA GET IT?

IT'S THE MOST PRECIOUS THING.

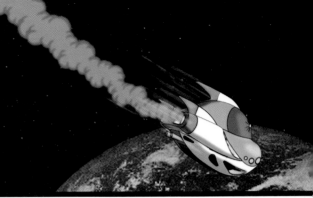

OH, THAT IS THE MOST *ADORABLE* THING I'VE EVER SEEN IN MY LIFE. YOU GUYS MADE A BANGO-RU DOLL?

MEAP.

HE *TALKS?*

WELL, MORE THAN FERB, BUT "MEAP" IS PRETTY MUCH THE ONLY THING HE SAYS.

WELL, YOU AND YOUR LITTLE *BANGO-ROBOT* BETTER NOT SHOW UP AT THE CONVENTION AND MAKE ME LOOK BAD!

MEAP.

OKAY! LET'S FIX US AN ALIEN SPACESHIP!

HEY, FERB, HAVE YOU SEEN PERRY?

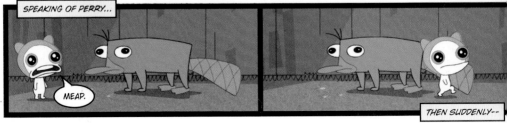

SPEAKING OF PERRY...

MEAP.

THEN SUDDENLY--

BACK IN THE YARD...

OH, HI, ISABELLA! WE'RE FIXING UP THIS SPACESHIP THAT BELONGS TO OUR NEW FRIEND, MEAP.

HI, GUYS. WHAT'CHA DOIN'?

HEH, HEH. MEAP.

HE'S THE MOST ADORABLE THING IN THE WORLD.

REALLY? ARE YOU SURE THERE'S NOTHING OR NO ONE THAT'S *MORE* ADORABLE?

NO. NOT A CHANCE.

HERE, SEE FOR YOURSELF. MEAP? *MEAP?*

OH, CANDACE! YOUR BANGO-RU! IT'S SO CUTE, I COULD *DIE!*

WHAT? OH, NO--

MEAP.

BANGO-RU!

BANGO-RU.

AND IT MAKES LITTLE NOISES! HOW DID YOU DO THAT?

OH, WELL, PHINEAS AND FERB, YOU KNOW?

OH, THEY TRICKED IT OUT FOR YOU. *COOL.* COME ON! LET'S GO TO THE CONVENTION.

RIGHT BEHIND YOU!

YOUR REIGN OF TERROR HAS COME TO AN END, SEÑOR FROWG!

OKAY, I RIGGED FERB'S OLD GPS DEVICE TO CREATE A *CUTE TRACKER.* IT LOCKS ONTO THE CUTEST THING IN THE AREA, SO IT *SHOULD* LEAD US RIGHT TO MEAP! *OOH,* I GOT SOMETHING!

OH, THAT'S PROBABLY ME. SORRY.

NO. IT'S THREE MILES IN *THAT* DIRECTION. WANNA COME AND HELP ME FIND MEAP?

SURE! I STILL HAVE TO GET MY YOU-WOULDN'T-KNOW-CUTE-IF-IT-BIT-YOUR-LEGS-OFF ACCOMPLISHMENT PATCH!

COOL! LET'S GO!

MEANWHILE, DOOFENSHMIRTZ EVIL, INC. IS CARPETED!

BLAST!

AH, PERRY THE PLATYPUS!

JUST IN TIME FOR YOUR LITTLE LESSON IN *STATIC ELECTRICITY!*

beep!

GRAB!

rub rub rub

FOOMP!

HA! IT LOOKS LIKE I RUBBED YOU THE WRONG WAY, *PUFFY THE FUZZYPUS!*

YOU MIGHT ASK--WHY THE CARPET? WHAT IS HE DOING? WHAT'S GOING ON? WHY IS HE LISTING QUESTIONS I MIGHT ASK HIM?

WELL, I BELIEVE THE ANSWERS ARE BEST EXPRESSED IN BACKSTORY FORM...

WHEN I WAS A BOY, I GOT A BALLOON AT A CARNIVAL. I DREW A FACE ON HIM. I SPRAYED HIM WITH A SPECIAL *LIFELONG* LASTING SPRAY I CREATED. AND I NAMED HIM *"BALLOONY."*

HE BECAME MY BEST FRIEND IN THE WHOLE WORLD... *YADA, YADA, YADA...* THEN ONE TRAGIC DAY WHEN I WAS PROTECTING OUR GARDEN AS A LAWN GNOME--

12

--WHATEVER, YOU REMEMBER *THAT* BACKSTORY-- BALLOONY STARTED FLOATING AWAY. I TRIED TO REACH OUT AND GRAB HIM, BUT I NEVER SAW BALLOONY AGAIN.

HE'S STILL OUT THERE SOMEWHERE. NOT TO PUT TOO FINE A POINT ON IT, BUT I PUT THAT *LONG-LASTING SPRAY* ON HIM, SO HE'S STILL AROUND!

AND I PLAN TO BRING HIM TO ME.

BALLOONS, YOU SEE, ARE DRAWN TO STATIC ELECTRICITY, SO I CREATED *THIS!*

BEHOLD THE STATIC-ELECTRO AMPLIFINATOR!

BUP, BUP, BUP, KEEP-KEEP BEHOLDING... KEEP BEHOLDING...BEHOLDING... AND WE'RE STILL BEHOLDING... AAAAND SCENE.

ELSEWHERE...

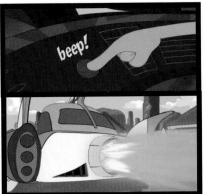

beep!

FWOOM!

MEANWHILE, NOT THAT DEEP IN SPACE...

WHAT'S THIS?

WARP-DRIVE SIGNATURE DETECTED.

HA-HA! I HAVE YOU NOW.

ELSEWHERE...

BANGO-RU!

THIS IS SO WEIRD.

IT'S LIKE A STRANGE ALIEN WORLD.

OOH, BANGO-RU PURSES! HOW CUTE!

I THINK I SAW THAT ONE ON THE RED CARPET THE OTHER NIGHT!

WHA--?
IRRESPONSIBLE
KIDS!

HEY! IS THIS *YOUR* DOLL, YOUNG LADY? I FOUND IT ABANDONED ON THE FLOOR OVER THERE. YOUR *IRRESPONSIBILITY* MAKES *MY* JOB AS SECURITY GUARD A MILLION TIMES HARDER!

I COULD HAVE TRIPPED OVER IT! YOU COULD HAVE KILLED ME! I'M LUCKY TO BE ALIVE!

YOU'RE IN *BIG* TROUBLE--

THE CUTE SIGNAL'S GETTING STRONGER. ALTHOUGH I KEEP GETTING THIS WEIRD CUTE INTERFERENCE FROM SOMEWHERE.

IT'S ME!
I'M ENDANGERING THE MISSION. I SHOULDN'T HAVE COME.

NO, IT'S MEAP'S SPACESHIP! WHOA, *SWEET!* YOU TRICKED IT OUT, FERB! ISABELLA AND I ARE HOT ON MEAP'S TRAIL. LET'S BOUNCE!

THEY CAN'T BAN ME FROM BANGO-RU CONVENTIONS FOR LIFE!

I BAN MYSELF!

AND WHAT KIND OF TOY *ARE* YOU, ANYWAY?

HEY, CANDACE, YOU FOUND MEAP!

UH, MORE LIKE HE FOUND ME...?

WELL, HIS SHIP'S FIXED, SO HE CAN GET BACK TO HIS FAMILY NOW!

ZAP!

WHAT'S HAPPENING?

GOTCHA!

WE'RE CAUGHT IN SOME KIND OF TRACTOR BEAM.

IT'S PULLING US IN! MAYBE IT'S THE SPACE AUTHORITIES. DID WE DO SOMETHING WRONG?

WELL, IT OCCURS TO ME THAT PERHAPS NOT **ALL** OF THE MODIFICATIONS I MADE ARE TECHNICALLY "STREET LEGAL."

WHAT'S GOING ON? **WAIT! COME BACK!** WHO WAS THAT?

THAT WAS YOUR FATHER?

MEAP.

OH, IT'S **NOT** YOUR FATHER? IT'S A MUG SHOT?

OH, NO! PHINEAS AND FERB HAVE BEEN ABDUCTED BY AN INTERGALACTIC CRIMINAL!

MEAP.

WHERE'S HE TAKING US?

LOOK, HE'S HEADED FOR THAT SMALL CLOUD.

THAT'S NO CLOUD. THAT'S A *SPACE STATION.*

I'VE GOT A GOOD FEELING ABOUT THIS!

Vrrrrm...

HA! YOU THOUGHT YOU WERE CLEVER DISGUISING YOUR SHIP, BUT I GOT YOU NOW...! WHOEVER...YOU... ARE...

HEY, LOOK, IT'S MEAP'S DAD!

ALL RIGHT, WHAT THE *HECK* IS GOING ON?! IS THIS SOME KIND OF *JOKE?*

I'M PHINEAS. THAT'S ISABELLA, AND THIS IS FERB.

WHAT'S *YOUR* NAME?

I AM KNOWN BY MANY NAMES THROUGHOUT THE UNIVERSE. WELL, *TWO* MAINLY--"MITCH" AND, UH, SOME OF THE GUYS CALL ME "BIG MITCH."

ANYWAY, WHERE'D YOU GET THIS SHIP?

IT'S MEAP'S SHIP... AND DON'T WORRY, HE'S JUST FINE.

OH, GOOD, GOOD...AND EXACTLY WHO IS "MEAP"?

WELL, THAT'S WHAT *WE* CALL HIM 'CAUSE IT'S ALL HE SAYS.

MEAP? ABOUT YEA HIGH, BIG EYES?

THE BIGGEST!

KINDA LOOKS LIKE THIS?

UPCOMING EVENTS

THAT'S MEAP!

THAT'S MY *MORTAL ENEMY!*

REALLY? HE SEEMS LIKE SUCH A NICE GUY.

HE IS! *I'M* NOT!

YOU SEE, I STEAL RARE CREATURES FROM THEIR HOME WORLDS AND IMPRISON THEM HERE ON MY SHIP. I'M A--

YOU'RE A *POACHER!* THAT'S *WRONG.* THESE POOR CREATURES SHOULDN'T BE LOCKED UP HERE! THEY SHOULD BE BROUGHT BACK TO THEIR HOMES AND SET FREE!

OH, *REALLY?* MAYBE I SHOULD LOCK YOU THREE UP IN HERE AS WELL.

NAH, THAT'S COOL. TONIGHT'S TACO NIGHT AT HOME!

MEANWHILE...

HI, MOM. PHINEAS AND FERB HAVE BEEN ABDUCTED BY AN EVIL ALIEN, AND I'M HERE WITH ANOTHER ALIEN WHO ISN'T HIS SON, AND--

HOW DOES THAT SOUND SO FAR?

I AGREE. CRAY-ZEE!

WHAT ARE WE GONNA DO?

PLAY CATCH?

HMM. WELL, IF YOU THINK IT'LL HELP.

PHINEAS AND FERB.

YOUR FATHER.

NO, RIGHT, NOT YOUR FATHER. A BAD GUY.

THEY'RE IN A GIANT SPACESHIP.

BUT HOW ARE WE SUPPOSED TO GET UP THERE AND SAVE THEM?

veep veep

OH, I GET IT!

DUH! YOU'RE TRYING TO TELL ME SOMETHING!

WHAT?

SO YOU KNOW WHEN YOU WALK AROUND IN SOCKS AND RUB THEM ON THE CARPET, YOU GET THAT LITTLE STATIC SHOCK?

BEHOLD THE NEW UNIFORM OF *PURE EVIL!* I CALL IT THE SOCKY SHOCKY SUITY.

ON SECOND THOUGHT...

OH, COOL! CHECK THESE CREATURES OUT!

WOULD YOU THREE SIT STILL? YOU DON'T GET IT. YOU'RE MY *PRISONERS!*

YOU SHOULD BE *AFRAID* OF ME!

AH, LIKE A MOTH TO THE FLAME.

YOU KIDS MIGHT BE OF SOME USE TO ME AF-- *HEY!* DON'T GO IN THERE! YOU'LL TRACK DIRT BACK INTO THE CORRIDOR!

ARGH! I'LL DEAL WITH THEM LATER!

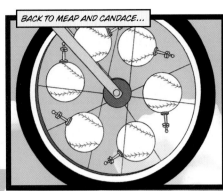

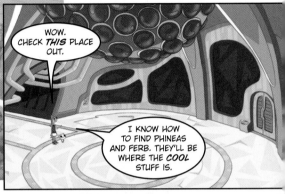

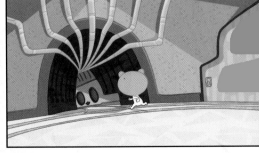

SO WE MEET AGAIN.

MEAP.

I AGREE. IT ENDS *HERE*.

OH, AND BY THE WAY, I TALKED TO YOUR LITTLE FRIENDS, AND JUST SO WE'RE CLEAR, I AM *NOT* YOUR FATHER!

OKAY, I'M ALMOST DONE CHARGING UP THE SOCKY SHOCKY SUITY SUIT.

zwip
zwip

YOU KNOW, IT'S THE TECHNICAL SIDE OF EVIL THAT I THINK PEOPLE DON'T REALLY APPRECIATE.

zwip

THERE! NOW WATCH AS EVERY BALLOON IN THE ENTIRE TRI-STATE AREA IS RIPPED FROM THE HANDS OF CHILDREN AND CLOWNS AND CLOWN CHILDREN!

CHARGE!

ARGH!

24

SUDDENLY--

MEAP!

OH, YEAH? WELL--

CRUNCH!

OH, MAN, WHAT THE--?

WE'RE RIGHT IN THE MIDDLE OF A SHOWDOWN, IF YOU DON'T MIND.

OH, OH, I GET IT. NEMESIS CONFRONTATION, EH? IT LOOKS SERIOUS. ONE OF THOSE "IT ENDS HERE" KIND OF THINGS...

HEH-HEH. NOT FUN.

WELL, DON'T MIND ME. I'M JUST "PLAYING" THROUGH, AS THEY SAY. I'LL SHOW MYSELF OUT.

beep!

NO, THAT'S WHERE I KEEP--

IT'S YOU!

BALLOONY!

HEY, THAT'S THE MOST UNIQUE CREATURE IN MY COLLECTION-- COLIN, MY BEST FRIEND.

WHAT? THAT'S BALLOONY, MY BEST FRIEND!

NO, I-I FOUND COLIN JUST FLOATING ALL ALONE IN SPACE.

WELL, I ACTUALLY DREW HIS FACE! LOOK, LOOK, I SIGNED IT!

Heinz

COLIN. *FEH!* COME ON, BALLOONY. LET'S SCOOT.

B-BALLOONY?

HA! SEE? COLIN IS *MY* BEST FRIEND!

YOU'VE *CHANGED*, BALLOONY! AND I THOUGHT YOU WERE ACTUALLY BACKSTORY-WORTHY! IT MAKES ME *SICK!*

WELL, I DON'T EVEN NEED YOU ANYMORE! YEAH, I'VE GOT AN EVEN *BETTER* BEST FRIEND!

HE'S A REALLY GOOD LISTENER. HE EVEN PUT UP WITH ME GOING ON ABOUT HOW GREAT YOU WERE. HA!

IT'S CLEAR TO ME NOW THAT MY *REAL* BEST FRIEND IS PERRY THE PLAT--

PUNCH!

AAAAIIEEE!!

UH, HELLO? FALLING TO MY DOOM HERE!

OH, *HI*, PERRY THE PLATYPUS! SEE? MY BEST FRIEND WILL SAVE ME...YOU ARE SAVING ME, RIGHT?

NOW THAT *THAT'S* OVER WITH...

beep!

SLAM!

ALL TOO EASY.

THAT WAS AWESOME!

I KNEW THERE WAS STILL MORE COOL STUFF TO DO IN SPACE!

UH-OH.

BOOM!

BOOM!

BOOM!

STRIKE THREE. THEY'RE OUT!

COOL! THANKS, CANDACE!

HEY, WHERE'S MEAP? I TOLD HIM TO WAIT RIGHT HERE.

I'LL TRY TO FIND HIM ON MY CUTE METER, BUT I'VE BEEN HAVING TROUBLE PICKING UP HIS CUTE SIGNAL.

PHINEAS, SINCE YOU OBVIOUSLY WON'T FIGURE THIS OUT ON YOUR OWN, I THINK *I'M* THE ONE CAUSING THE CUTE INTERFERENCE.

DON'T BE SILLY, ISABELLA.

I TOOK INTO ACCOUNT YOUR CUTENESS AND ADJUSTED THE SETTINGS FROM THE BEGINNING! SEE, LOOK WHAT HAPPENS IF I CHANGE IT BACK TO NORMAL...

OOPS. SO MUCH FOR FINDING MEAP.

DO YOU THINK HE'S OKAY?

NO. NO, DON'T.

FOOLISH CHILDREN. ONLY NOW DO YOU UNDERSTAND YOUR GRAVE SITUATION.

MEAP!

HI, MITCH!

"HI, MITCH! LOOK AT THE COOL STUFF, MITCH! BLAH, BLAH, BLAH, MITCH!"

I MEAN, SERIOUSLY? SERIOUSLY? YOU'RE *STILL* NOT GETTING THIS? YOU'RE ALL TRAPPED ON MY SHIP FOREVER, LIKE ANIMALS IN A CAGE! *GET IT?* YOU *LOST!* I *WON!*

veep!

BONK!

MEAP.

HUH?

WHAM!

OOF!

MEAP!

CHILDREN, *THANK YOU* FOR YOUR HELP IN BRINGING DOWN THIS *VILLAINOUS SCOUNDREL.*

YOU SEE, I AM AN *INTERGALACTIC SECURITY AGENT* WHO ROAMS THE UNIVERSE...

...*BUSTING* PEOPLE WHO DO STUFF THEY'RE NOT SUPPOSED TO DO.

YOU'RE LIKE THE *ME* OF THE GALAXY!

TH